ANIMAL ANTICS A TO Z

Quentin Quokka's Quick Questions

by Barbara deRubertis • illustrated by R.W. Alley

KANE PRESS / NEW YORK

Alpha Betty's Class

Alexander Anteater

Bobby Baboon

Corky Cub

Dilly Dog

Eddie Elephant

Frances Frog

Gertie Gorilla

Hanna Hippo

Izzy Impala

Lana Llama

Jeremy Jackrabbit

Kylie Kangaroo

Maxwell Moose

STAR of the BOOK

Nina Nandu

Oliver Otter

Polly Porcupine

Quentin Quokka

Rosie Raccoon

Sammy Skunk

Tessa Tiger

Umma Ungka

Victor Vicuna

Walter Warthog

Xavier Ox

Yoko Yak

Zachary Zebra

Alpha Betty

Text copyright © 2011 by Barbara deRubertis
Illustrations copyright © 2011 by R.W. Alley

Series Editor: Juliana Hanford
Book Design: Edward Miller

Library of Congress Cataloging-in-Publication Data

deRubertis, Barbara.
Quentin Quokka's quick questions / by Barbara deRubertis ; illustrated by R.W. Alley.
p. cm. — (Animal antics A to Z)
Summary: Quentin Quokka's questions help out during school when an earthquake strikes during
a concert.
ISBN 978-1-57565-338-9 (library binding : alk. paper) — ISBN 978-1-57565-329-7 (pbk. : alk. paper)
[1. Curiosity—Fiction. 2. Schools—Fiction. 3. Earthquakes—Fiction 4. Quokka—Fiction. 5. Alphabet.]
I. Alley, R. W. (Robert W.), ill. II. Title.
PZ7.D4475Qu 2011
[E]—dc22   2010025290

ISBN 978-1-57565-381-5 (e-book)

5 7 9 10 8 6 4

Kane Press

An imprint of Boyds Mills & Kane, a division of Astra Publishing House

www.kanepress.com

Printed in China

Animal Antics A to Z is a registered trademark of Astra Publishing House

Quentin Quokka was always asking questions.
Quick little questions. Quiet little questions.
Questions. Questions. Questions!

Quentin asked Mama and Papa
LOTS of questions.
"If you squeeze a squash, is it
squishy or squashy?"

"If you tickle a worm, will it
squiggle and squirm?"

Quentin asked even MORE questions at school.
"I have a quick question," he would say.

Alpha Betty, his teacher, would smile.
"You ask a LOT of questions, Quentin.
But they're good questions!"

One day Alpha Betty took her class to
the aquarium.

A guide pointed out a squid in a big tank.

Of course, Quentin had a question.
"Do squid really squirt ink?" he inquired.

Just then a big fish started chasing the squid.

Quick as a wink, the squid squirted a cloud
of inky black liquid!
Then it squiggled away and hid.

Quentin giggled. "I think the answer to my question is YES!"

The next week Alpha Betty took the class to visit Queenie Quail's Quince Jam Factory.

Queenie showed the class her quince trees. And she showed them how to make jam from the fruit.

Quentin stood close to Queenie so he could
watch the pot of jam cooking.

"I have a quick question," he squeaked.
"Is quince jam supposed to SMOKE?"

"QUAAACK!" said Queenie when she looked
at the pot. "We must add more liquid!"

Quentin quickly filled a quart jar with water.
And Queenie poured it into the pot.
The jam *hissed* loudly!

When it quieted down, Queenie added some spices. She tasted the jam . . . and smiled!

"I think we've just created something new!" she said. "Our first pot of Quentin Quokka's Smoky Quince Barbeque Sauce!"

Then came the most exciting day of all.
Quincy Quoll's world-famous Quart Jar Quartet
was coming to visit Alpha Betty's class!

Quentin loved the quartet's songs—
especially "The Squiggle Wiggle Boogie"!

Alpha Betty had a request for Quentin.
"The quartet can't spend much time with
us today. So please try not to ask questions.
Just listen and enjoy the music!"

Quentin nodded.

Suddenly Quincy Quoll banged the door open!
"Are you kids ready to boogie?" he boomed.

"Yes!" the class squealed.

The quartet quickly set out their quart jars.
They added water up to a mark on each jar.
Then they tested the tones of the jars by
tapping them: PING, PANG, PONG.

Quentin had LOTS of questions. But he kept quiet.

Finally the Quart Jar Quartet put on fancy
jackets covered with sequins.
They picked up their sticks.

And Quincy Quoll said, "Uh-one! Uh-two!
Uh-one-two-three-four!"

The quartet's sticks were flying!
The music ROCKED as they struck the jars.
This made the jars shiver and shake.
It made the liquid quiver and quake.

In fact, EVERYTHING was quivering and
quaking!

Suddenly Quentin jumped up.

"I have a quick question!" he squeaked.
"Are we having an earthquake?"

The quartet stopped playing.
But the quivering and quaking did not stop.

"Drop, cover, and hold on!" said Alpha Betty.
"Quickly now!"

The class ducked under their desks.
The quartet squeezed under their tables.
They all held on to something.

After a few moments, the quaking quit.
Everything was quiet.

Alpha Betty said, "It's safe to come out now.
The earthquake is over!
We're lucky it was a small one!"

Quincy Quoll came over to Quentin.
"Who is this quick-thinking student?" he asked.

Alpha Betty smiled proudly.
"This is Quentin Quokka.
He always asks the BEST questions!"

"Now I have a question for YOU, Quentin," said
Quincy. "Would you like to request a song?"

"Oh, yes!" said Quentin."Please play
'The Squiggle Wiggle Boogie'!"

Quincy Quoll grinned. "Excellent choice!"

The quartet grabbed their sticks, and Quincy
said, "Uh-one! Uh-two! Uh-one-two—"

"One quick question!" Alpha Betty interrupted.
"Quentin, can you teach us how to do
'The Squiggle Wiggle Boogie'?"

Quentin beamed. "You bet I can!"

The quartet started playing a wild boogie-woogie.
And Quentin Quokka sang and danced along!

"Make your arms squiggle and wiggle!
Make your legs shiver and shake!
*Do the boogie-woogie like you're in an **earthquake**!*
Squiggle . . . wiggle . . . boogie!"

Soon everyone was doing "The Squiggle
Wiggle Boogie." Even Alpha Betty!

Afterwards, Quentin Quokka had
one . . . last . . . question:

"Could we please
do it again?"

FUN FACTS

- Home: Quokkas (pronounced "**kwok**-uhs") live in Western Australia.
- Family: Quokkas are in the same family as wallabies and kangaroos. A baby quokka stays in its mother's pouch for months after it's born.
- Appearance: Quokkas are about the size of a housecat. They have small, rounded bodies with thick brown and grey fur.
- Food: Quokkas mainly eat grass and leaves and feed at night. They are very sociable, and as many as 150 will gather at a water hole. But they are able to go for months *without* water!
- **Did You Know?** Quokkas can hop on their two hind feet OR walk on all four feet!

LOOK BACK

Learning to identify letter sounds (phonemes) at the beginning, middle, and end of words is called "phonemic awareness."

- Remember that *q* and *u* are friends who always stick together! *Qu* sounds like *kw*.
- The word *question* <u>begins</u> with the *qu* sound. Listen to the words on page 23 being read again. When you hear a word that <u>begins</u> with the *qu* sound, make your arms squiggle and wiggle while you say the word!
- Listen to the words on page 29 being read again. If you hear the *qu* sound <u>anywhere</u> in a word, make your legs shiver and shake while you say the word!
- **Challenge:** Chant the words and dance to "The Squiggle Wiggle Boogie" on page 29!

TRY THIS!

Quincy Quoll's Quart Jar Words

- Draw 6 quart jars like Quincy Quoll's and cut them out.*
- Write each of the following letters or pairs of letters on a jar: a **green** *qu*, a **red** *i*, a **black** *ck*, a **black** *ll*, a **black** *t*, and a **black** *z*.
- Now you're ready to make words! Put the **green** *qu* jar first, the **red** *i* jar in the middle, and a **black letter** jar last. Sound out the word you made. What does it mean? Can you use it in a sentence?
- Now change the **black letter** jar to each of the other 3 in turn, and repeat the last step!

*A printable, ready-to-use activity page with 6 quart jars is available at: www.kanepress.com/AnimalAntics/QuentinQuokka.html

FOR MORE ACTIVITIES, visit www.kanepress.com.